For Charlie
— H.M.Z.

For my sister, Cheryl
— N.W.

Text copyright © 2011 by Harriet Ziefert
Illustrations copyright © 2011 by Noah Woods
All rights reserved / CIP Data is available.
Published in the United States 2011 by
Blue Apple Books, 515 Valley Street, Maplewood, NJ 07040
www.blueapplebooks.com
First Edition   09/11 Printed in Shenzhen,China
ISBN: 978-1-60905-089-4

2 4 6 8 10 9 7 5 3 1

PUPPY IS LOST

by Harriet ZIEFERT
art by Noah WOODS

Blue Apple Books

Max's puppy is lost.

She was here and now she is gone.

"Come for dinner!" called Max.

Puppy thought,

Max looked everywhere for Puppy.

Under the bushes . . .

behind the
trash bins . . .

and near the sandbox.

But he could not
find Puppy anywhere.
He walked home alone.

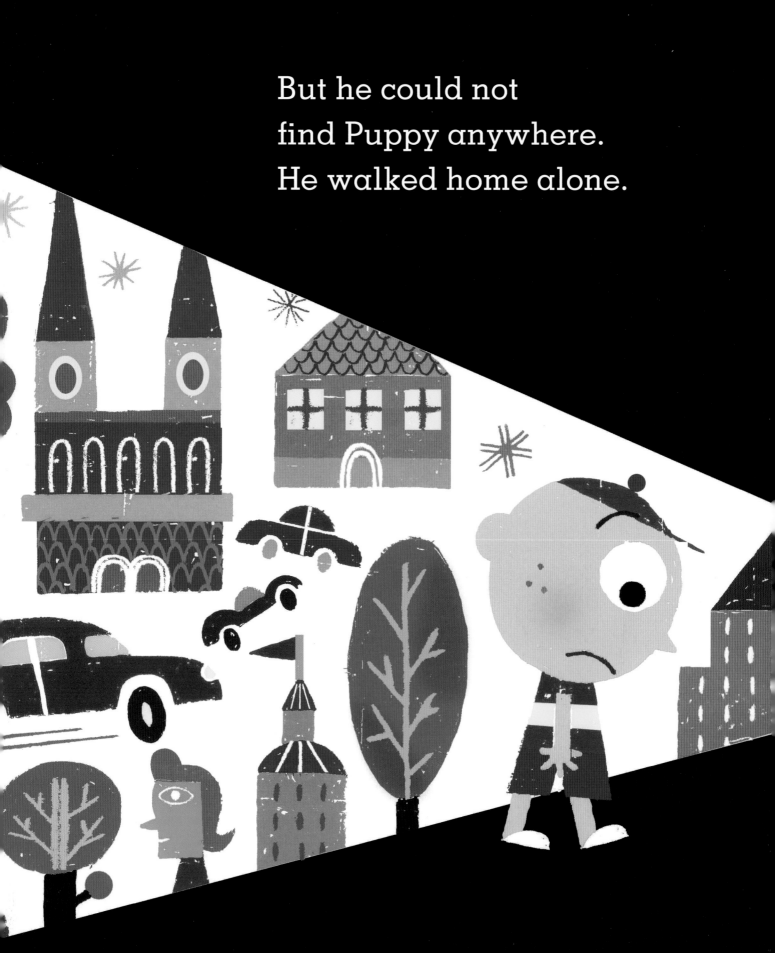

Max had no appetite.
He could not even eat dessert.

In the middle of the night,
Max had a scary dream.
He could not go back to sleep.

Max got out of bed
and sat down at his desk.

He made "Lost Dog" posters.
Lots of them.

I LOST MY DOG

HER NAME IS PUPPY!

SHE IS SMALL & BROWN & FRIENDLY

HAVE YOU SEEN MY DOG? I REALLY MISS HER. SHE IS NOT JUST AN ORDINARY PUPPY. SHE IS MY BEST FRIEND.

IF YOU SEE MY PUPPY PLEASE CALL ME. MY NAME IS MAX. MY DOG IS PUPPY & SHE LOOKS LIKE THIS: CALL 704-1960

Max hung the posters near his house and near the park.

Then he walked home.

Puppy wandered in circles. But she couldn't find Max.

Max was sad. And lonely.
He waited for news
of his lost dog.

He waited . . .

and waited.

RINGGG!!

RING!!!

RING!!

Then the phone rang.
But the call was for Dad.
It was not news
about Puppy.

When the doorbell rang,
it was Max's friend, Lucy.
Max told her Puppy was lost.

"I'll help you look for her,"
said Lucy.

"Okay," said Max.
"Let's look for Puppy in the park."

There were lots of dogs in the park.

But none of them were lost.

"I have an idea," said Max.

"Let's go to where I last saw Puppy.
We can just wait there."

Puppy was tired of wandering.
She thought,

I'M GOING BACK TO THE SPOT
WHERE I LAST SAW MAX.

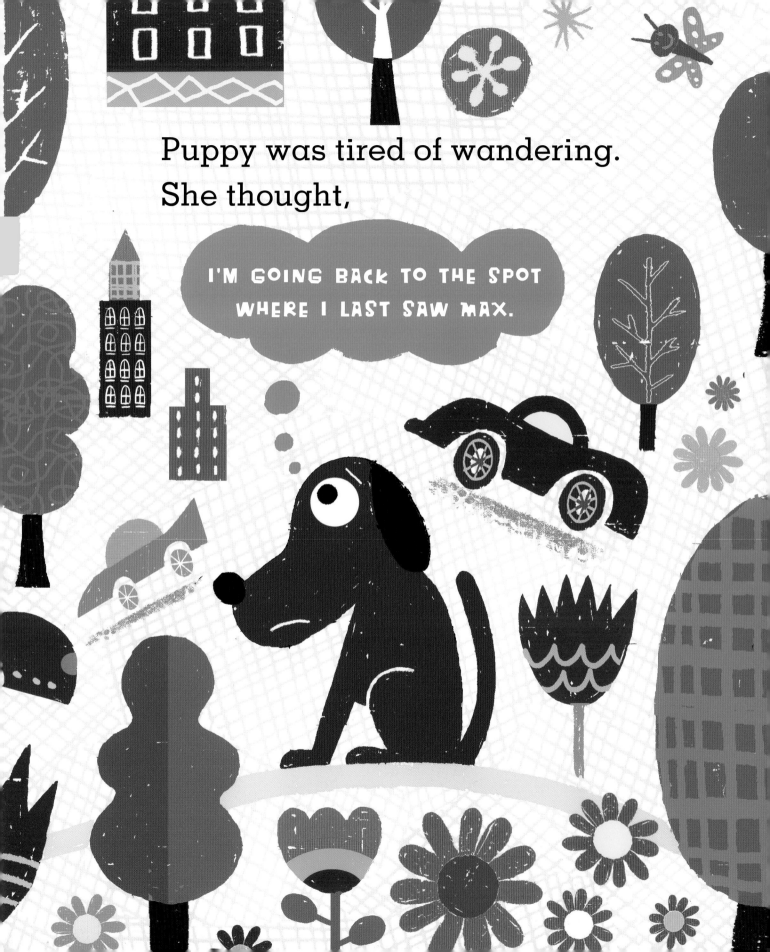

Max waited for Puppy.

Puppy waited for Max.

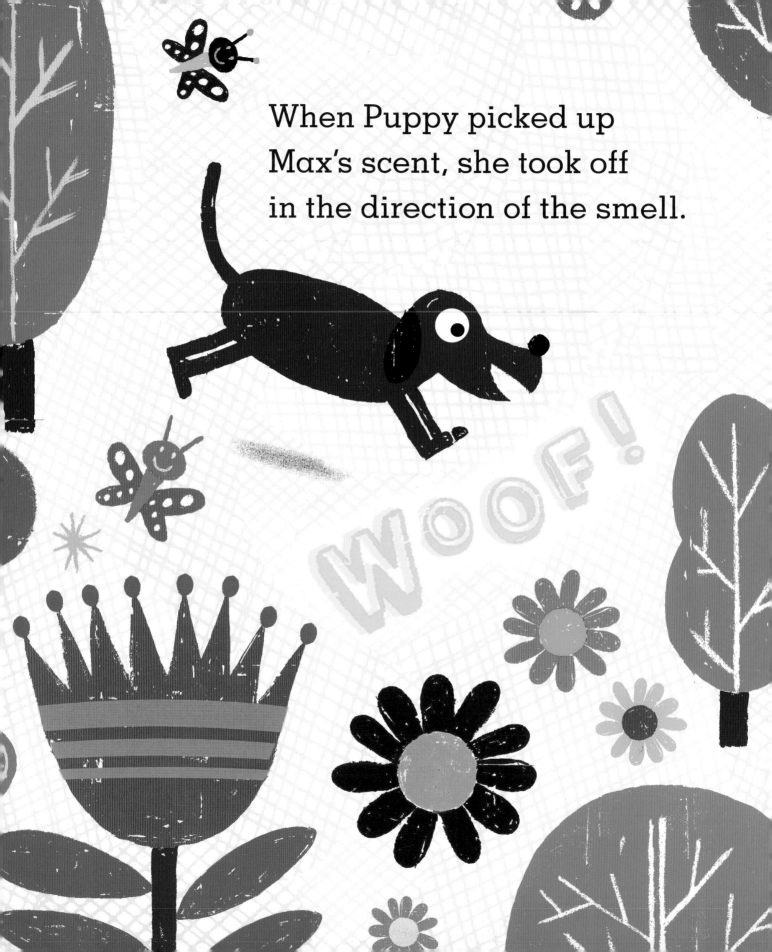

When Puppy picked up
Max's scent, she took off
in the direction of the smell.

WOOF!

Max recognized Puppy's bark
and ran to meet her.

"Now you're not a lost puppy," said Max.

"You are found!"